Each letter has a poem. Every poem is a clue. The answers

HOLIDAY HOUSE / New York

L T
ABET

by **LESA CLINE-RANSOME**

illustrated by **JAMES E. RANSOME**

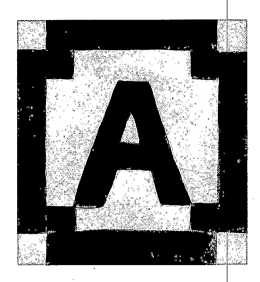

Red, green, and golden hues

Nature's handpicked treat

Wholesome goodness to the core

Each bite a savory sweet

A perch above the world below

A private bird's-eye view

A roomy home if just for one

A cozy nest for two

Spotted in a pasture green

Holsteins spend their days

Lazing, gazing, chewing, mooing,

Gathered for a graze

Cloth, yarns, buttons,
and lace

Stitched with joy
and tears

Keepers of most
treasured secrets

Shared throughout
the years

E

Gathered by the dozen

Stacked with loving care

Nestled in a basket

Favorite breakfast fare

A garden of late bloomers

Showered with autumn's rays

Carpet a lawn with color

To brighten chilly days

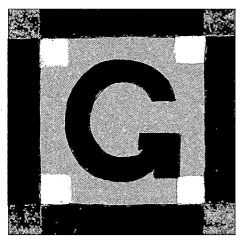

An ornamental invitation

To the world within

A welcome with wide-open arms

Invites the outside in

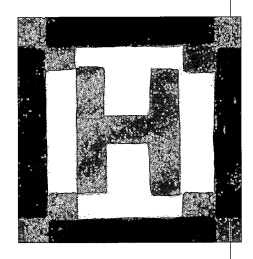

A rocking, rollicking romp

A sideways, saddled stomp

Rodeo rider or out on the plain

Home again on his own terrain

From the soil a slow advance

In leafy, lengthy lines

Sprouting leaves along the way

On intertwining vines

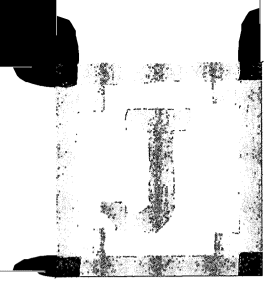

Haunted smiles, toothless grins

The pumpkin masquerade begins

Warning tricksters of their fate

Candy-coated treats await

A pot brimming with promise

A whistling, boiling brew

Captures the cold under its lid

And warms you through
and through

The last bright spots of autumn

Ablaze with fiery light

Wave to the wind a fond farewell

Before their feathery flight

Spoken with pen and hand

Across the miles, throughout the land

Connections from near and away

Tucked in a secret hideaway

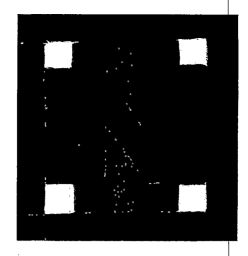

As the sun lies down
  for an evening nap

And the day begins to fade

The moon and stars come out
  to play

And the sky pulls
  down the shade

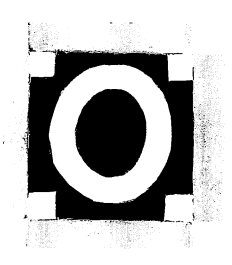

Sweeping the sky, searching the ground

Wings outstretched, eyes shiny and round

A nightbird draped on an evening flight

Hunting for prey by the glow of moonlight

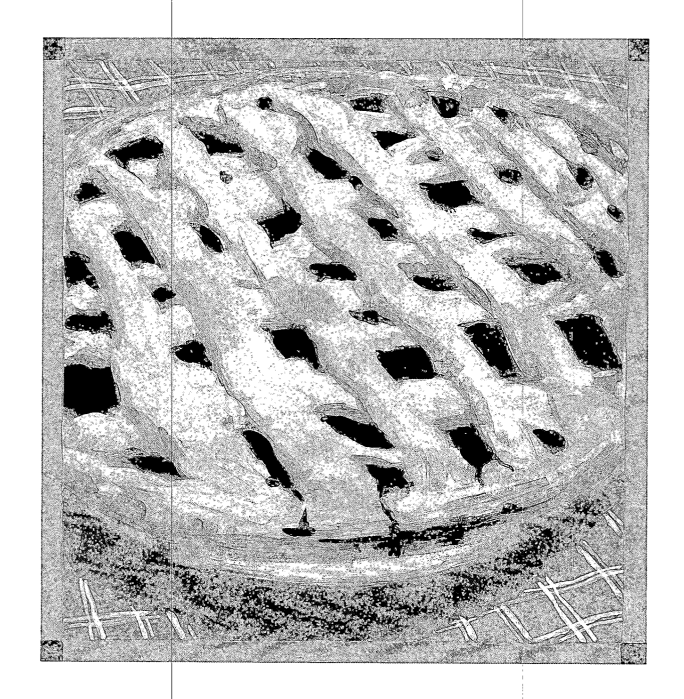

One part sugar, two parts spice

Baked inside each sweet slice

Seasoned with love, sprinkled with care

Fresh-baked fragrance fills the air

A patch of you, a scrap of me

Pieces of family history

Common threads stitched from the heart

Pieces of us in every part

Cock-a-doodle-doo
　How do you do?

Open your sleepy eyes

Cock-a-doodle-doo
　How do you do?

A solo at sunrise

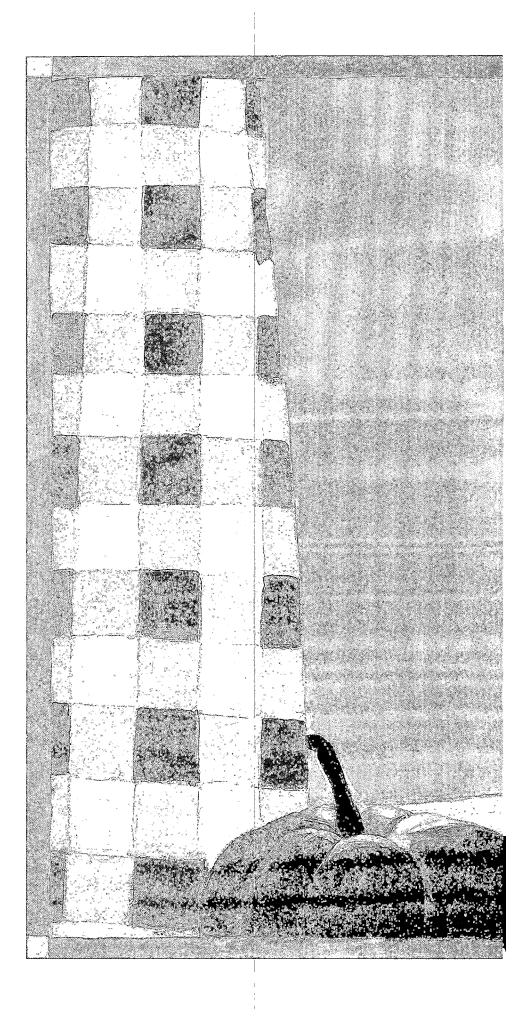

S

From a burlap sack, some sticks, and hay

A looming figure grows

The lonely farmer stands alone

No time to sit and doze

Push Pull Plow Plant

Trudging through the land

Heave Haul Heft Heap

A farmer's helping hand

Beneath a blanket of sun

A canopy striped bright

A lunch table set in shade

From the noon daylight

A recipe for fall

In a potpourri of flavor

Fresh treasures bronzed with autumn light

Tastes for all to savor

Memories of long ago

Now weathered by the sun

Of Sunday visits, hayrides,

And days filled with fun

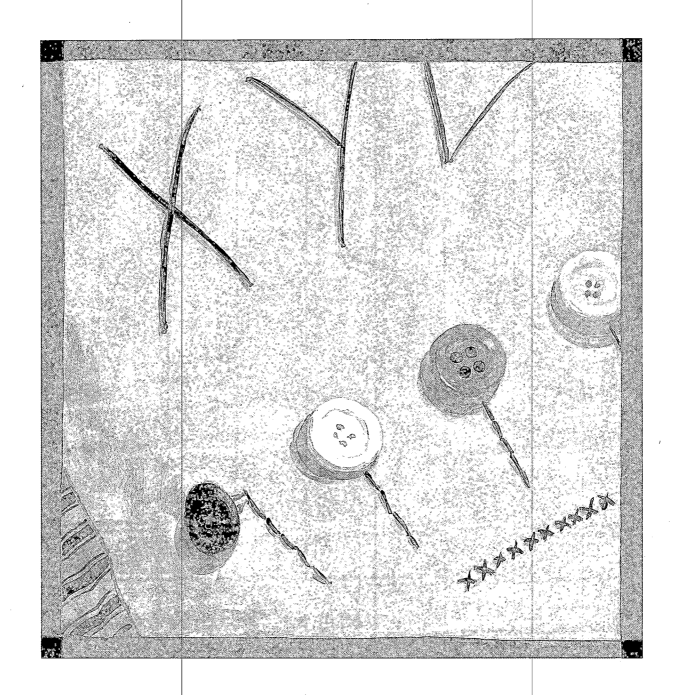

Baste a cloth with needle and thread

Letter stitch by stitch

The simplest of samplers

Humble homes enrich

Y

Soaked with sun

Ripened with rays

A cascade of color

Dapples the days

Never-ending turns

Turning left then right

The path that leads
   to everywhere

And then right out of sight

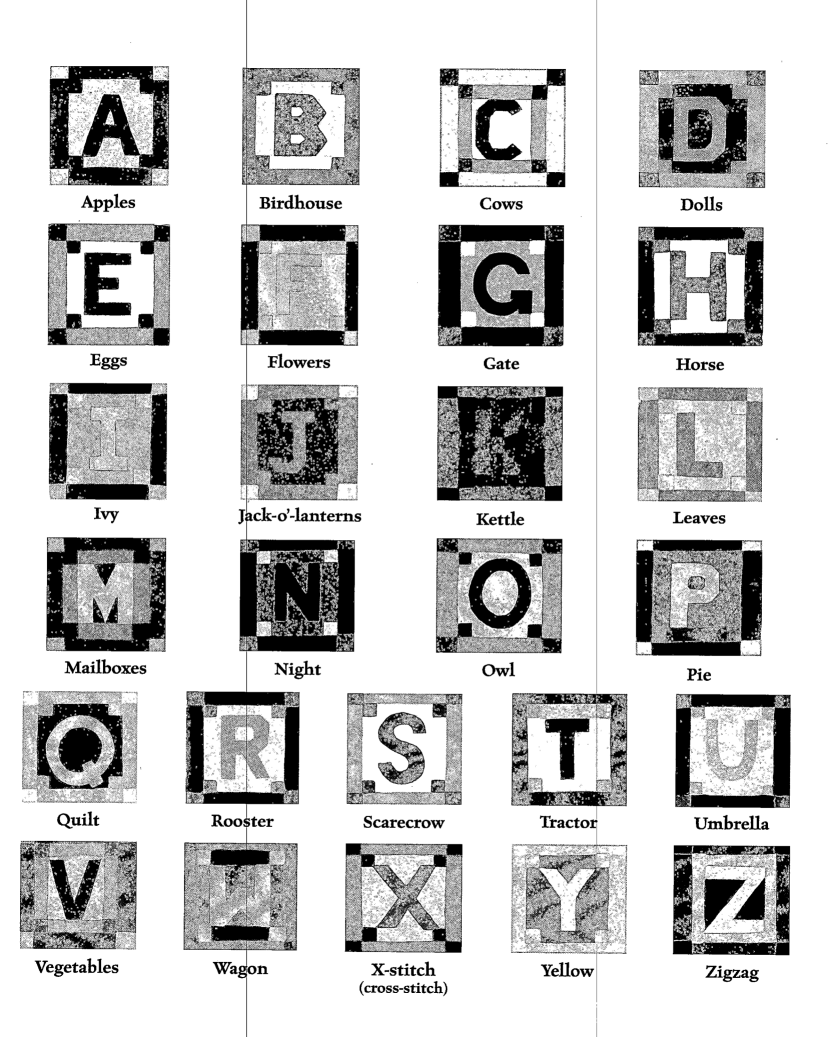

Apples

Birdhouse

Cows

Dolls

Eggs

Flowers

Gate

Horse

Ivy

Jack-o'-lanterns

Kettle

Leaves

Mailboxes

Night

Owl

Pie

Quilt

Rooster

Scarecrow

Tractor

Umbrella

Vegetables

Wagon

X-stitch
(cross-stitch)

Yellow

Zigzag

To my sister, Linda

L. C.-R.

To my Sweet Pea, Leila

J. E. R.

Library of Congress Cataloging-in-Publication Data

Cline-Ransome, Lesa.
Quilt Alphabet / by Lesa Cline-Ransome;
illustrated by James E. Ransome.—1st ed.
p. cm.
ISBN 0-8234-1453-1 (hardcover)
1. English language—Alphabet—Juvenile poetry.
2. Country life—Juvenile poetry.
3. Children's poetry, American.
[1. Country life—Poetry. 2. American poetry.
3. Alphabet.] I. Ransome, James, ill. II. Title.

PS3603.L56 Q55 2001
811'.6—dc21
2001016588